D1333283

For David and Mary Wild
E.R. & P.R.

To Ginny and Catherine
for all their help
R.B.C.

First published 1991 by Walker Books Ltd
87 Vauxhall Walk, London SE11 5HJ

Text © 1991 Emma & Paul Rogers
Illustrations © 1991 Robin Bell Corfield

First printed 1991
Printed and bound in Hong Kong by
South China Printing Co. (1988) Ltd

British Library Cataloguing in Publication Data
Rogers, Paul &Emma
Zoe's tower.
I. Title II. Corfield, Robin Bell
823'.914[J]
ISBN 0-7445-1547-5

ZOË'S TOWER

Written by

Paul and Emma Rogers

Illustrated by

Robin Bell Corfield

WALKER BOOKS
LONDON

If you leave
the warm house
and follow the path,

you come to a leafy lane.

If you go along the lane
and a little bit further,

you come to a wooden gate.

And if you climb over the wooden gate
and march up the muddy track,

you come to a shady wood.

And if you go through the shady wood,
   past where the best blackberries
   hang just out of reach,
   where pheasants flap up startled,

you come to a sunny meadow.

And if you cross the sunny meadow,
   where lapwings go tumbling up into the air,
   where the stream disappears, gurgling,

you come to the place
where Zoë's tower stands.

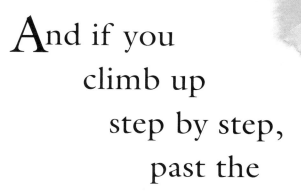

And if you
climb up
step by step,
past the
scuttling spider,
past the slit where
the wind whistles
and the ledge with
the empty nest,

you come out under the sky
where the crows wheel and dive.

And if you stand on tiptoe,

you can see the whole way that you came...

and a little bit further.

And if you listen,
in the wind you can hear
someone calling,

And then
you know

that it's time
to go…

home.